A Note to Parents

For many children, learning math is difficult and "I hate math!" is their first response — to which many parents silently add, "Me, too!" Children often see adults comfortably reading and writing, but they rarely have such models for mathematics. And math fear can be catching!

The easy-to-read stories in this **Hello Math Reader!** series were written to give children a positive introduction to mathematics and to give parents a pleasurable reacquaintance with a subject that is important to everyone's life. **Hello Math Reader!** stories make mathematical ideas accessible, interesting, and fun for children. The activities and suggestions at the end of each book provide parents with a hands-on approach to help children develop mathematical interest and confidence.

Enjoy the mathematics!
• Give your child a chance to retell the story. The more familiar children are with the story, the more they will understand its mathematical concepts.
• Use the colorful illustrations to help children "hear and see" the math at work in the story.
• Treat the math activities as games to be played for fun. Follow your child's lead. Spend time on those activities that engage your child's interest and curiosity.
• Activities, especially ones using physical materials, help make abstract mathematical ideas concrete.

Learning is a messy process and learning about math calls for children to become immersed in lively experiences that help them make sense of mathematical concepts and symbols.

Although learning about numbers is basic to math, other ideas, such as identifying shapes and patterns, measuring, collecting and interpreting data, reasoning logically, and thinking about chance are also impor   . By reading these ries and having fun with the activi   hild enthusiastically say, "Hello, ma   h."

—Marilyn F
National Mathematics Educator
Author of *The I Hate Mathematics! Book*

*For my mother, who taught me to love reading,
and my father, who taught me to love pizza.*
— C.A.L.

For my dahling husband, Steve.
— J.S.

ISBN 0-439-30473-3

Copyright © 2002 by Scholastic Inc.

The activities on pages 27–32 copyright © 2002 by Marilyn Burns.
All rights reserved. Published by Scholastic Inc.
SCHOLASTIC, HELLO MATH READER, CARTWHEEL BOOKS, and
associated logos are trademarks and/or registered trademarks of Scholastic Inc.

Library of Congress Cataloging-in-Publication Data available

10 9 8 7 6 5 4   05 06

Printed in the U.S.A.   23
First printing, January 2002

PIZZA PIZZAZZ!

by Carol A. Losi
Illustrated by Jackie Snider
Math Activities by Marilyn Burns

Hello Math Reader! — Level 3

SCHOLASTIC INC.
New York   Toronto   London   Auckland   Sydney
Mexico City   New Delhi   Hong Kong   Buenos Aires

Mario the Pizza Man baked
pizza every night at Pizza Planet.
"I will bake the perfect pizza for you,"
Mario told all his customers.
"I have every topping in the universe.
What would you like on your pizza?"
People always ordered plain cheese pizzas.

"Cheese! Cheese! How can I bake
a perfect pizza if I only use cheese?" Mario asked.
"Tonight *I* will choose the toppings.
Tonight I will bake perfect pizzas!"

Two customers came into Pizza Planet.
Mario the Pizza Man looked at them
carefully, up, down, and all around.
Before they could say, "Cheese pizza, please,"
Mario said, "Have I got a pizza for you!"
He ran to the kitchen.

Mario rolled the dough, spread
the sauce, and sprinkled the cheese.
"I will start with an easy pizza," he said.
He put pepperoni on one-half of the pizza.
He put sausage on the other half.
When the pizza was done,
Mario the Pizza Man served it to . . .

... two teenagers.

"Yo, Mario," they said.
"This is the perfect pizza for us."

Three new customers came into Pizza Planet.
Mario looked at them carefully,
up, down, and all around.
He thought and thought.
"I have every topping in the universe," he said.
"Have I got a pizza for you!"

Mario rolled the dough, spread the sauce,
and sprinkled the cheese.
He put hamburgers on one-third of the pizza.
He put hot dogs on one-third of the pizza.
He put marshmallows on one-third of the pizza.
Then Mario lit the pizza on fire.

When the pizza was done,
Mario the Pizza Man served it to . . .

… three firefighters.

"You're hot, Mario!" they said.
"This is the perfect pizza for us."

Four new customers came into Pizza Planet.
Mario looked at them carefully,
up, down, and all around.
He thought and thought.
Then he smiled and said,
"I have every topping in the universe.
Have I got a pizza for you!"

Mario rolled the dough, spread the sauce, and
sprinkled the cheese.
He put clams on one-fourth of the pizza.
He put squid on one-fourth of the pizza.
He put crab on one-fourth of the pizza.
He put dried seaweed on one-fourth of the pizza.
When the pizza was done,
Mario the Pizza Man served it to . . .

... four fishermen.

"Way to go, Mario," they said.
"This is the perfect pizza for us."

Five new customers came into Pizza Planet.
Mario looked at them carefully,
up, down, and all around.
He thought and thought.
"I have every topping
in the universe," he said.
"Have I got a pizza for you!"

Mario rolled the dough, spread the sauce,
and sprinkled the cheese.
He put corn on one-fifth of the pizza.
He put beans on one-fifth of the pizza.
He put squash on one-fifth of the pizza.
He put sprouts on one-fifth of the pizza.
He put potatoes on one-fifth of the pizza.
When the pizza was done,
Mario the Pizza Man served it to . . .

... five farmers.

"You're the best, Mario," they said.
"This is the perfect pizza for us."

Six new customers came into Pizza Planet.
Mario looked at them carefully,
up, down, and all around.
He thought and thought.
"Welcome!" he said.
"At Pizza Planet I have
every topping in the universe.
Have I got a pizza for you!"

Mario rolled the dough, spread the sauce, and
sprinkled the cheese.
He put popcorn on one-sixth of the pizza.
He put cotton candy on one-sixth of the pizza.
He put peanuts on one-sixth of the pizza.
He put lollipops on one-sixth of the pizza.
He put bubble gum on one-sixth of the pizza.
He put snow cones on one-sixth of the pizza.
When the pizza was done,
Mario the Pizza Man served it to . . .

... six clowns.

"Three cheers for Mario," they said.
"This is the perfect pizza for us."
One of them honked his horn.

Eight new customers came into Pizza Planet.
Mario looked at them carefully,
up, down, and all around.
He thought and thought.
"I have every topping in the universe," he said.
"Have I got a pizza for you!"

Mario rolled the dough, spread the sauce, and
sprinkled the cheese.
He put olives on one-eighth of the pizza.
He put sausage on one-eighth of the pizza.
He put bacon on one-eighth of the pizza.
He put chicken on one-eighth of the pizza.
He put lamb on one-eighth of the pizza.
He put liver on one-eighth of the pizza.
He put steak bones on one-eighth of the pizza.
He put dog biscuits on one-eighth of the pizza.
When the pizza was done,
Mario the Pizza Man served it to . . .

... a woman and her seven dogs.

"Thank you, Mario," she said.
"This is the perfect pizza for us."
The dogs barked.

By now it was late.
Pizza Planet was ready to close.
Some new customers came in.

Mario the Pizza Man stared
up, down, and all around.
He wasn't even sure how many
new customers he saw.
Mario thought and thought
and thought and thought.
Finally, he scratched his head and said,
"I'm sorry. I thought I had
every topping in the universe.
But I do **NOT** have a pizza for you."

"Perhaps you should change your sign,"
said the new customers.
Then they walked out to their spaceship.

Mario the Pizza Man quickly changed his sign
and locked his door.
"Have I got a pizza for *me*!" he said.
Then he made one last pie for his dinner—
a plain cheese pizza.

And it was perfect!

More Pizza Sharing

How would you share three pizzas among four people?

Cut out three paper "pizzas." Divide them so each person gets the same amount.

How much pizza will each person get?

Now divide five pizzas among four people. Then try to share six pizzas among four people.

If your child is particularly interested in these problems, present more by changing the number of pizzas or the number of people. For example: How would you share three pizzas among six people? Two pizzas among three people?

A Pizza for Two People

Two customers ordered a pizza cut into four equal-sized pieces, each with a different topping: sausage, pepperoni, mushrooms, and onion. Each customer ate two pieces.

One customer said, "I ate two-fourths of the pizza."

The other customer said, "I ate one-half of the pizza."

Mario said, "You're both right."

What do you think?

Listening to your child's response is a way to assess his or her understanding. Don't worry if your child isn't sure of the answer. He or she may need more time and experience to learn about the important idea of equivalent fractions.

A Pizza Party

Mario was making pizza for four people. He decided to make two small pizzas. Figure out how to share them equally.

Draw two paper "pizzas" on paper by using the top of a paper cup or glass to trace circles.

Use your scissors to cut the pizzas so each person gets the same share.

How much pizza will each person get?

Some children cut each pizza into four pieces and give each person two pieces. Others, cut each pizza in half and give each person one piece. Both solutions are correct. Whichever method your child uses, show him or her the other way. This can help a child see that one-half is the same as two-fourths.

Fancy Fraction Words

The top number of a fraction is called the **numerator**. The bottom number is called the **denominator**.

Can you say these words?

The **numerator** of one-fourth is 1.

The **denominator** of one-fourth is 4.

Which is a bigger piece of the same-sized pizza: $\frac{1}{2}$ or $\frac{1}{3}$? Explain why.

Which is a bigger piece of the same-sized pizza: $\frac{1}{4}$ or $\frac{1}{8}$?

Which is a bigger piece of the same-sized pizza: $\frac{1}{5}$ or $\frac{1}{2}$? Compare other pizza slices.

Pick a Perfect Pizza

Mario made another new sign for Pizza Planet.

Mario used fractions to show one-half, one-third, one-fourth, one-fifth, one-sixth, and one-eighth. Can you read the fractions on Mario's sign?

Here's a hint: Each fraction has two numbers. The 1 on top refers to one piece of pizza. The number on the bottom tells how many equal-sized pieces are in the whole pizza.

Retelling the Story

Why did Mario decide that he would choose the toppings for people's pizzas instead of letting them decide?

Who were the two customers who came into Pizza Planet together? Mario divided their pizza into two equal-sized pieces. What did he put on each half? Do you think this was a perfect pizza for them?

Who were the three new customers who came into Pizza Planet together? Mario divided their pizza into three equal-sized pieces. What did he put on each third? Do you think this was a perfect pizza for them?

Ask yourself the same questions about Mario's groups of four, five, six, and eight new customers.

Why didn't Mario have any ideas for the last customers who came into Pizza Planet? What ideas do you have for toppings Mario could have put on their pizza?

What kind of pizza did Mario make for himself?

It's common to hear children say, "My half is bigger than your half." However, a key idea that children must learn is that fractional parts of the same whole are the same size. In the examples above, emphasize that all the slices on the same pizza are the same size.

• ABOUT THE ACTIVITIES •

Fractions have a reputation for being difficult to understand and hard to learn. This doesn't have to be so. What's important when teaching fractions is to help children lift the concepts off the pages of math books and bring them to life. Instruction should give children opportunities to make sense of fractions.

One effective way to teach about fractions is to connect them to real-world experiences. This story does just that. Presenting different options for pizza toppings and cutting pizzas into different numbers of pieces are perfect contexts for introducing the idea of fractional parts of a whole. After enjoying the story, the activities in this section help children think about fractions and learn about the standard symbolism used to represent them.

School math instruction focuses on fractions in grades four and up, but the best time to introduce children to fractions is in earlier grades, before fractions become a high-stakes topic. Children benefit from informal experiences with fractions that develop understanding in a relaxed and enjoyable manner while building children's interest in and curiosity about fractions.

After enjoying the story with your child, use these activities to extend their understanding of and comfort with fractions.

Have fun doing the math!

—Marilyn Burns

You'll find tips and suggestions
for guiding the activities whenever
you see a box like this!